Tea Time!

The Irish drink more cups of tea per person than any other people in the world! Although tea is drunk throughout the day, afternoon tea is usually enjoyed between 3:00 and 6:30. Tea taken with milk and sometimes sugar is often accompanied by tomato, ham or egg sandwiches, soda bread and butter, chocolate biscuits, and teabrack, an Irish fruit cake.

Magpies

Impressive black and white birds, magpies belong to the crow family. They are the most common bird in Ireland. The magpie is a noisy, chattering bird. It has a high-stepping gait and hops and bounces along when excited. Traditionally, to see one magpie is unlucky; to see two promises joy.

Soda Bread

A quick and easy soda bread is made daily in Ireland. It can be made with white or wholemeal flour. When made with wholemeal it is called brown bread. Here is a traditional recipe from County Mayo:

    4 cups flour
    I tea_____
    I tea_____
    2 cup_____

Mix into a dough and kn_____
on a floured baking shee_____
bread is best eaten the _____

Visitors

The word *failte* is Irish for welcome, and in Ireland visitors are always welcome. Tourism is an important industry for the hospitable and friendly Irish. Sights in Ireland include rugged seacoasts, lush valleys, old-fashioned villages, castles, cottages, early Christian churches, and ancient ruins. Burrishoole Abbey, pictured on page 11, was built around the year 1450.

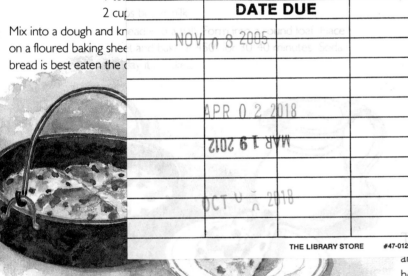

Pigs

Pigs, also called hogs or swine, were one of the first domesticated animals. A source of meat, leather, and other products, pigs live happily indoors and outdoors. A sow — an adult female — usually gives birth to litters of eight to twelve piglets. Pigs have small eyes, and they cannot see very well, but they have a great sense of smell and root for food with their big snouts. Pigs are said to be very intelligent. Some people say that happy pigs have curly tails like Molly's.

Collies

Collies have been bred to help farmers herd their flocks of sheep, and the black and white Border Collie can be seen throughout Ireland. A very intelligent, crafty, and sometimes quick-tempered breed, these dogs manage many sheep over wide areas. Sheepdogs are trained not to hurt the sheep.

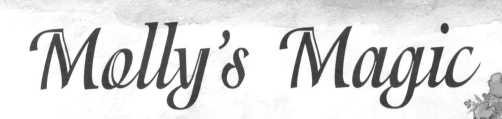

Molly's Magic

Written by **Penelope Colville Paine**

Illustrated by **Itoko Maeno**

MarshMedia, Kansas City, Missouri

For my parents, Donald and Joan Wallington

Special thanks to
Elisabeth Nielson of the California Polytechnic State University Swine Unit,
Maureen McGovern, Maureen McGee, Peter McGee,
Mick and Sheila McDonald, Sue and Richard Steer, the Hanrahan family,
Carol Talley, Mindy Bingham, Cheryl Coons, Jayne Caldwell,
and the residents of Newport, County Mayo, Ireland.

Text ©1995 by Marsh Film Enterprises, Inc.

Illustrations ©1995 by Itoko Maeno

Published by **MARSH**media

    A Division of Marsh Film Enterprises, Inc.
    P. O. Box 8082
    Shawnee Mission, KS 66208

Library of Congress Cataloging-in-Publication Data
Paine, Penelope Colville.
    Molly's magic/written by Penelope Colville Paine;
illustrated by Itoko Maeno.
       p.   cm.
    Summary: Molly, a clever pig living on an Irish farm, helps supplement
the family income by attracting customers to their tea garden. Endpapers
present information about Ireland and about farm life and farm animals.
    ISBN 1-55942-068-5
    [1. Pigs—Fiction. 2. Farm life—Ireland—Fiction.
3. Ireland—Fiction.] I. Maeno, Itoko, ill. II. Title.
PZ7.P163Mo 1995   94-48491
[Fic]—dc20

Book layout and typography by Cirrus Design

Printed in Hong Kong

O'MALLEY'S farm overlooked Clew Bay. While the sheep wandered over the rugged farmlands and the cows grazed in the clifftop pasture, a family of pigs dozed comfortably in the muddy barnyard sty. All except a special pig named Molly.

Molly was at home in the farmhouse kitchen, where young Miles O'Malley had taken care of her since she was little, feeding her warm goats' milk and mashed potatoes. Molly liked to sleep in her spot by the turf fire or lie in the doorway watching Paddy the farmhand as he worked in the yard.

But the best time of the day was when Miles came home from school.

Miles was special too. He knew all kinds of magic and tricks, and every day he would teach Molly something new — how to find hidden apples, dance a jig, or balance a tin plate on her head.

"Watch Molly do a trick, Mum," Miles said one afternoon as he pretended to pull a handball from Molly's ear. He tossed the ball in the air, and Molly caught it neatly.

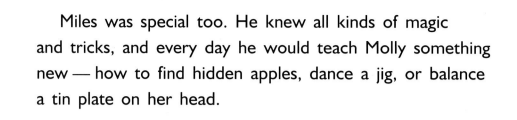

"Why is this pig still in my kitchen?" Grace O'Malley exclaimed as she tripped over Molly. "Perhaps for her next trick she could make herself disappear." She opened the back door and pushed Molly outside with the broom.

Molly's days in the kitchen were over, but she didn't care. She played handball with Miles against the side of the barn and rode to town with him in the bucket of the tractor.

She learned to swim and to help Dougal the sheep dog herd the sheep. She stayed out of Mrs. O'Malley's way.

One afternoon Molly was napping in the rose garden when she was awakened by strange crunching noises.

She opened one eye, then the other, and to her amazement she saw sheep, lots of sheep, busily munching on Mrs. O'Malley's beans and pansies.

Molly jumped to her feet. She wondered where Dougal was, but the sheep were crowding into the garden and there was no time to spare. What if they ate all the roses?

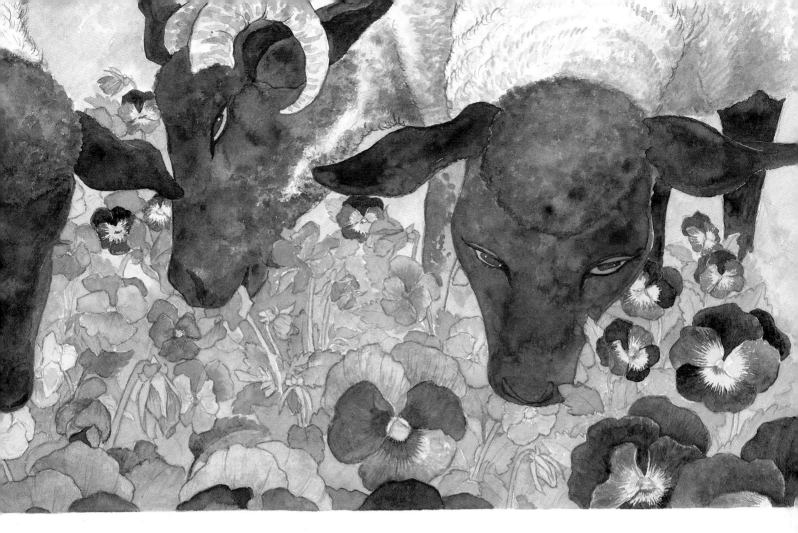

Molly remembered Dougal's commands, and with an oink and a squeal she herded the bleating sheep across the yard towards the old abbey where they scurried through the gap in the wall. Molly was close on their tails, so busy giving instructions that she did not notice that the gap was meant for sheep . . . but not for pigs.

Molly was stuck tight. "Perhaps if I kick my trotters," she thought, "I could push myself back." But that didn't work. There had to be a way.

Then it started to rain, and for Molly rain meant mud. "Aha! That might just do the trick!" she nodded to herself. And it did. Her dusty body soon became slippery and muddy with the rain water, and with a few twists and turns she slithered out.

"The culprit!" Mrs. O'Malley exclaimed, spotting Molly as she entered the yard. "I've been looking for you!" Mrs. O'Malley turned on the tap and started to hose Molly down, calling to Paddy for help.

"My word," said Paddy. "She does scrub up well! Are you taking her somewhere?"

"Yes I am," Mrs. O'Malley answered. "She has eaten all my beans, not to mention my pansies. I have enough problems without wondering where she is or what she is doing. It is time for Molly to join her sisters in the sty."

Molly found it very hard to be in the sty, especially under such unjust circumstances. Her sisters, Breda and Maureen, were not very creative. Set in their routine, they would just eat, roll, and sleep. They grunted in annoyance when Molly caught the apples Miles threw to her. They snorted in disgust when she danced around the trough and, worst of all, they made fun of her curly tail. Their tails, of course, were perfectly straight.

To pass away her time Molly would lean over the sty wall and watch what was going on around the house and barn. One sunny morning Paddy set out tables, chairs and pretty umbrellas in the garden while Mrs. O'Malley painted a sign.

Farmfresh Teas
2:00 – 5:00 every afternoon
O'Malley's Seaside Farm
Plenty of Parking

Miles placed the sign by the gate and tied a balloon to the top.

"I wish more visitors would come for tea," Miles confided to Molly one evening, giving her some leftover cakes. "We didn't serve many people today, and Mum says she needs to make a profit to help buy feed for the winter. We are listed in the tourist guide book, and Mum made a sign, but the

problem is not enough tourists see the sign. What do you think, Molly?" he asked. "Do you have any ideas? Paddy says we need a magician to conjure up some customers."

Molly thought hard about this problem all night.

In the morning she asked the cows if they knew where the tourists stayed. "Nooo," they answered, plodding along. "We only go to the field and back. That's all we know."

Molly asked the sheep if they had seen any tourists. "Oh we really wouldn't know," they answered all together. "We don't notice much. We just follow each other around."

"You fly around and chatter to everyone," Molly said to the magpies. "Do you know where I can find tourists?"

"Straight over there past the hay field on the main road," one magpie answered hurriedly, pointing towards the sky with a wing, "but as you only have legs you will have to go up the lane!"

"Hmmm . . ." said Molly. "Thanks a lot." Now she had the information she needed. Now she had to think of a way to get out of the sty . . . then she would need to move the sign . . . and then . . . she gazed out over the hay field deep in thought.

For once, Molly was glad her sisters stuck rigidly to their daily schedule. She could be sure they would settle into their afternoon nap just after lunch. As they snored loudly, their big bodies shuddering up and down, Molly dug herself out of the sty. She had found a soft spot by the gate. And she had a plan.

"I think it will work," she smiled to herself, heading for the lane.

Molly poked her nose between the hinged
sides of the tea sign and wriggled underneath.
A perfect fit! She hurried along the lane,
past the hay field.

The main road was busy with holiday traffic. Molly positioned herself in good view of all the passing cars. Every now and then, she spun around to make sure everyone could see the sign.

First one car and then another turned down the lane. Molly grinned and waved a trotter. It seemed that her idea was working.

Miles and Mrs. O'Malley had to rush around to keep up with the customers. They even had to ask Paddy to help. "More soda bread," called out Miles, "and another dish of cream!"

"I can't believe we're so busy," Mrs. O'Malley said. "It's like magic!"

"Such a clever sign!" said a visitor. "Why, that pig of yours is irresistible! I had to come and see your farm, and I'm glad I did. This tea is delicious!"

"Pig?" said Mrs. O'Malley, looking towards the sty. "What pig?"

"Why the one with the sign . . . the one at the corner of the main road . . . the one waving." As he spoke, in trotted Molly, sign and all, followed by three more carloads of customers.

"Molly!" Miles exclaimed. "I knew it! It's not really magic, Mum. It just seems that way. It's Molly's magic — her good thinking. She found a solution to our problem!"

"And she's found food," the tourist added, pointing to Molly, who was making her way toward the table, hungry after her hard work. "Pleased to meet you, Miss Molly," he chuckled, holding out an eclair. "Now I wonder, have you ever thought of flying?"

"Hmm," smiled Molly, looking up at the sky. "I might just do that!"

Dear Parents and Educators:

Good ideas seem like magic to those who haven't learned to think problems through and find solutions. Our children need to learn how to make this "magic" if they are to become productive citizens of the twenty-first century. Their confidence and success depend upon it. Indeed, the future of the world depends upon it.

When we teach boys and girls to confront challenges with their heads as well as their hearts, to be inquisitive, to ask questions, and to explore options, we equip them with skills for facing the demands of their futures.

Children must be given opportunities to develop their thinking skills. We need to promote the exercise of their minds just as actively as we encourage the exercise of their bodies. And we must guard against inadvertently discouraging creative thinking. The boy or girl who asks "Why?" and "What if?" and "What else?" may tax the time and energy of teachers and caregivers, but questions like these come from problem-solvers in the making.

Help children understand Molly's message by asking these questions:

- When did Molly first begin to learn new things?
- How did Molly learn to herd sheep?
- What problem with the tea garden did Miles share with Molly?
- Did Molly know a solution to the problem right away? How did she find a solution?
- What happened when Molly stood by the road with the tea sign on her back?
- Can you think of a problem in your life that needs a solution?

Here are some ways to help children think about problems:

- Ask them to clarify the problem and to state it in a brief sentence.
- Encourage them to restate the problem in terms of a goal to be reached.
- Help them think of steps they could take to achieve the goal.
- If there is more than one approach to solving the problem, encourage them to consider the advantages and disadvantages of each approach.
- Model an open mind about possible solutions to problems. Even unsuccessful ideas can be useful, leading to a right answer or a revised approach.
- Introduce brain teasers to help children practice thinking skills and have fun doing it!

Available from MarshMedia

Storybooks — Hardcover with dust jacket and full-color illustrations throughout.

Videos — The original story and illustrations combined with dramatic narration, music, and sound effects.

Activity Books — Softcover collections of games, puzzles, maps, and project ideas designed for each title.

Bailey's Birthday, written by Elizabeth Happy, illustrated by Andra Chase. 32 pages. ISBN 1-55942-059-6. Video. 18:00 run time. ISBN 1-55942-060-X.

Clarissa, written by Carol Talley, illustrated by Itoko Maeno. 32 pages. ISBN 1-55942-014-6. Video. 13:00 run time. ISBN 1-55942-023-5.

Gumbo Goes Downtown, written by Carol Talley, illustrated by Itoko Maeno. 32 pages. ISBN 1-55942-042-1. Video. 18:00 run time. ISBN 1-55942-043-X.

Hana's Year, written by Carol Talley, illustrated by Itoko Maeno. 32 pages. ISBN 1-55942-034-0. Video. 17:10 run time. ISBN 1-55942-035-9.

Jomo and Mata, written by Alyssa Chase, illustrated by Andra Chase. 32 pages. ISBN 1-55942-051-0. Video. 20:00 run time. ISBN 1-55942-052-9.

Kiki and the Cuckoo, written by Elizabeth Happy, illustrated by Andra Chase. 32 pages. ISBN 1-55942-038-3. Video. 14:30 run time. ISBN 1-55942-039-1.

Kylie's Concert, written by Patty Sheehan, illustrated by Itoko Maeno. 32 pages. ISBN 1-55942-046-4. Video. 17:20 run time. ISBN 1-55942-047-2.

Kylie's Song, written by Patty Sheehan, illustrated by Itoko Maeno. 32 pages. (Advocacy Press) ISBN 0-911655-19-0. Video. 12:00 run time. ISBN 1-55942-021-9.

Minou, written by Mindy Bingham, illustrated by Itoko Maeno. 64 pages. (Advocacy Press) ISBN 0-911655-36-0. Video. 18:30 run time. ISBN 1-55942-015-4.

Molly's Magic, written by Penelope Colville Paine, illustrated by Itoko Maeno. 32 pages. ISBN 1-55942-068-5. Video. 16:00 run time. ISBN 1-55942-069-3.

My Way Sally, written by Mindy Bingham and Penelope Paine, illustrated by Itoko Maeno. 48 pages. (Advocacy Press) ISBN 0-911655-27-1. Video. 19:30 run time. ISBN 1-55942-017-0.

Papa Piccolo, written by Carol Talley, illustrated by Itoko Maeno. 32 pages. ISBN 1-55942-028-6. Video. 18:00 run time. ISBN 1-55942-029-4.

Pequeña the Burro, written by Jami Parkison, illustrated by Itoko Maeno. 32 pages. ISBN 1-55942-055-3. Video. 18:00 run time. ISBN 1-55942-056-1.

Tessa on Her Own, written by Alyssa Chase, illustrated by Itoko Maeno. 32 pages. ISBN 1-55942-064-2. Video. 15:00 run time. ISBN 1-55942-065-0.

Time for Horatio, written by Penelope Paine, illustrated by Itoko Maeno. 48 pages. (Advocacy Press) ISBN 0-911655-33-6. Video. 19:00 run time. ISBN 1-55942-026-X.

Tonia the Tree, written by Sandy Stryker, illustrated by Itoko Maeno. 32 pages. (Advocacy Press) ISBN 0-911655-16-6. Video. 12:10 run time. ISBN 1-55942-019-7.

You can find storybooks at better bookstores. Or you may order storybooks, videos, and activity books direct by calling MarshMedia toll free at 1-800-821-3303.

MarshMedia has been publishing high-quality, award-winning learning materials for children since 1969. To receive a free catalog, call 1-800-821-3303.

Ireland

The island of Ireland is located in northwestern Europe. The first settlers arrived in Ireland about 6000 B.C., and in the following centuries Celts, Vikings, English, and many other peoples struggled to gain control of the island. Today Ireland includes the Republic of Ireland, an independent country, and Northern Ireland, a part of the United Kingdom. Molly's story takes place in the western part of the Republic of Ireland, in County Mayo — one of 26 counties in the republic.

UNITED KINGDOM
of GREAT BRITAIN
and NORTHERN IRELAND

EUROPE

NORTHERN IRELAND

Derry
Belfast

Clew Bay
Newport
Galway
Dublin
REPUBLIC of IRELAND
Shannon
Waterford
Cork

Irish Tin Whistle

The tin whistle, like the one played by Miles O'Malley, is a popular instrument in Ireland. Also called the penny whistle, the tin whistle is inexpensive and easy to play, and it is a favorite souvenir for children to take home from Ireland. Other traditional Irish instruments are the harp, fiddle, Irish bagpipes, accordion, and *bodhran,* a type of drum.

Symbols of Ireland

The most famous symbol of Ireland is the shamrock. It is said to be lucky to find one with four leaves. The official symbol of the Republic of Ireland is the harp, a popular Irish instrument for hundreds of years. The green, white, and orange flag of the republic represents unity between Ireland's Roman Catholics and Protestants.

Peat Fires

About 10% of Ireland is covered with peat bogs, the result of decaying prehistoric forests in the cold, wet Irish climate. Throughout time the Irish have used this natural resource as a fuel, and anyone who visits Ireland will remember the distinctive smell of turf (peat) burning. The peat is traditionally cut by hand with a tool called a "slane." The brick-shaped pieces are stacked to dry and stored for use.

Sheep

Sheep farming for wool is the primary farming activity in the western part of Ireland. Sheep roam the rugged hillsides grazing on grass and wild plants. Gaps in stone walls, sometimes called "sheep passes" allow sheep to graze from field to field. A natural all-weather fabric, wool protects the Irish people from the cold rain that often falls without warning. Irish hand knitting is prized the world over.

Cattle

Cattle and dairy cows are also part of the Irish farm. Although sheep raising is more common in the western part of Ireland, in other parts of the country, cows are far more numerous.